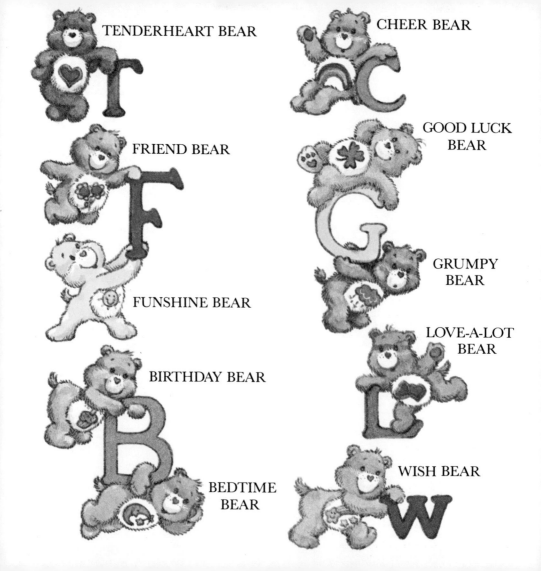

TENDERHEART BEAR

CHEER BEAR

FRIEND BEAR

GOOD LUCK
BEAR

FUNSHINE BEAR

GRUMPY
BEAR

LOVE-A-LOT
BEAR

BIRTHDAY BEAR

WISH BEAR

BEDTIME
BEAR

The Care Bears' Book of ABC's

by Peggy Kahn

illustrated by
Carolyn Bracken

A Care Bear Book™ from Random House, New York

Copyright © 1983 by American Greetings Corporation. Care Bear and Care Bears are trademarks of American Greetings Corporation. All rights reserved under International and Pan-American Copyright Conventions. Published in the United States by Random House, Inc., New York, and simultaneously in Canada by Random House of Canada Limited, Toronto.

Library of Congress Cataloging in Publication Data: Kahn, Peggy. The Care Bears' book of ABC's. "A Care Bear book from Random House, New York." Summary: The Care Bears introduce the letters from A to Z. 1. Alphabet rhymes. [1. Bears—Fiction. 2. Stories in rhyme. 3. Alphabet] I. Title. PZ8.3.K12425Car 1983 [E] 82-18538 ISBN 0-394-85808-5 (trade); ISBN 0-394-95808-X (lib. bdg.) Manufactured in the United States of America 2 3 4 5 6 7 8 9 0

The Care Bears will take you
from A to Z.

They hope you'll have fun
with the letters you see!

A is for airplane,
high in the sky.

B

B is for balloons
 the Care Bears fly!

C is for cakes
that Birthday
Bear bakes.

He writes
Happy Birthday

on each one
he makes.

D

D is for daisies
that Friend Bear will pick
to bring to someone who is sick.

E

E is for Easter eggs
—blue, pink, and green—
that hide a licorice jellybean!

F is for fish
in a babbling brook
that steal the bait
on a Care Bear's hook.

G is for the garden gate,
where the Care Bears
sometimes wait.

H is for hugs.
Care Bears give just enough,

packed with kisses and cuddles
and lots of good stuff!

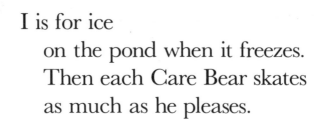

I is for ice
        on the pond when it freezes.
Then each Care Bear skates
        as much as he pleases.

J is for jack-o'-lanterns,
    shining bright,
    that might scare a Care Bear
    on Halloween night!

K is for kite,
caught in a tree.

Grumpy Bear's angry!
He can't get it free!

L is for lemons
    to make lemonade,
    a cool drink for hot days
    to sip in the shade.

M is for the moon
that crosses the sky
while Bedtime Bear sings
a soft lullaby.

N

N is for nuts
Care Bears find in the fall
and share with the squirrels,
who like nuts best of all!

O is for orchestra—
woodwinds and strings.
Tenderheart dances
and Friend Bear sings!

P is for parties
with presents and prizes
and packages Cheer Bear
has filled with surprises.

Q is for quilt,
spread on a bed.
It warms a snoozing
sleepyhead.

R is for rainbows
the Care Bears ride
and use just like a
slippery slide.

S

S is for the sun
that makes a
fine day.

T is for the train
that chug-chugs away.

U is for umbrella
to use when it rains.
"My umbrella won't work!"
Grumpy Bear complains.

V is for valentines
from Love-a-Lot Bear.
They're her way of saying
"I really care!"

W is for wishing well.
Toss in a penny!
Then make a wish,
if you have any.

X is for xylophone.
Each bar is a note.
A plink of a hammer
and out the sounds float!

Y is for yo-yo,
  a toy that will please...and

Z zips
up our ABC's!

Your trip through the alphabet's
come to a close,
And the Care Bears are happy
because they suppose

That while you've been learning
about each letter
You've gotten to know
the Care Bears better.